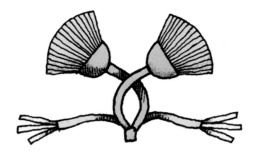

Bill and Pete

STORY AND PICTURES BY

Tomie de Paola

Penguin Young Readers Group

FOR
BERNICE,
MARGARET,
& ALICE,
WHO WERE THERE
WHEN IT ALL STARTED.
♡ t.

Library of Congress Cataloging-in-Publication Data   dePaola, Tomie. Bill and Pete.
Summary: When William Everett Crocodile is chosen to be a suitcase,
his talking toothbrush becomes his salvation.
1. Crocodiles—Fiction   I. Title. PZ7.D439Bi   E   78-5330
ISBN 978-0-698-11400-5
37 38 39 40

William Everett Crocodile lived on the banks of the River Nile with his mama.

One day, Mama said, "William Everett, now that you have nice crocodile teeth, we must go to Mr. Hippo's store and get you a toothbrush before you start school tomorrow."

William Everett liked Mr. Hippo's store because it was full of things. He and Mama walked up one aisle and down another.

They stopped in front of the toothbrush counter. "You may choose your own toothbrush, William Everett," Mama said.
William Everett looked and looked.

"Hi!" said a toothbrush. "What's your name?"
"My name's William Everett. What's yours?"
"Pete," said the toothbrush.

"I found the toothbrush I want, Mama,"
said William Everett. "His name is Pete."
"Good," said Mama. "We can go home now."

So Pete became William Everett's toothbrush.
And his best friend, too.

The next morning Mama said, "William Everett, wake up. It's time to go to school."

"Oh, Mama," William Everett said. "I can't wait to read and write and learn all about crocodile history."

"Someday, I will be proud of you, William Everett," Mama said.

"Now, class," said Ms. Ibis. "Today, we are going to learn the alphabet. Then we will be able to write our names. Now, repeat after me...."

The little crocodiles repeated after Ms. Ibis. "A–B–C–D–E–F–G...."

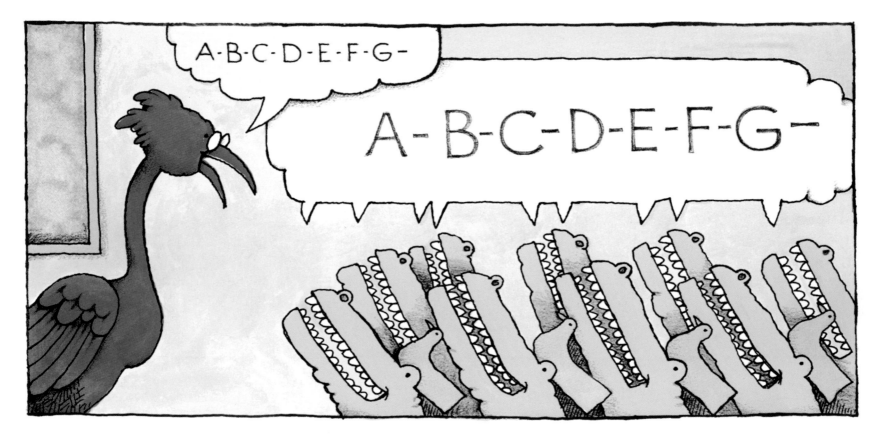

They said the whole alphabet.

They said the letters over and over again until they knew all of them by heart.

"Well, William Everett," said Mama. "What did you learn in school today?"
"William Everett, say the alphabet," said Pete. William Everett said every letter without a mistake.

"Oh, William Everett," Mama said. "That was beautiful."

The next day, Ms. Ibis taught the class how to write all the letters.

The little crocodiles wrote the letters over and over until they could write them by heart.

"And what did you learn today, William Everett?" Mama asked.

"William Everett, write the letters," said Pete.

William Everett wrote every letter without one mistake.

"You're so smart, William Everett," Mama said.

"Someday, you will be famous."

"Today, class, we are going to write our names," said Ms. Ibis.

She showed all the little crocodiles just what letters each one had in his or her name.

They wrote and wrote and wrote and smiled and smiled and smiled.

The letters spelled out: Sam–Jane–John–Kay–Kate–Tom–Amy....

They all wrote and smiled some more.

All except William Everett. He had so many letters
in his name that he kept forgetting at least one of them.

Poor William Everett.
Big tears ran down his nose.

"Is something wrong, William Everett?"
Pete asked.
"I'll never learn how to write my name,"
he cried. "It has too many letters."

"Now, now, William Everett," said Pete.
"I think I can help you to write your name
and not forget any letters."
He took a pencil and wrote.

"Did you learn something today, William Everett?" asked Mama.

"Yes, Mama, I learned to write my name," said William Everett.

"Oh, Bill." Mama beamed.

One Saturday, when there was no school, Bill and Pete went down to the River Nile and sat on the bank in the sun. A man on a bicycle went riding by.

Behind the bicycle were cages filled with crocodiles.

"I wonder what *that's* all about?" said Bill.

"That's the Bad Guy, and those crocodiles
are on their way to Cairo–to become suitcases,"
said an old crocodile swimming by. "Watch out
he doesn't catch you!"

But he did. The very next Saturday.
Bill and Pete were fishing and they didn't
hear the Bad Guy creep up behind them.

The Bad Guy lassoed Bill and put him in a
cage. He didn't pay any attention to Pete.
Pete tried to peck the Bad Guy, but Pete was
just too small.

Poor Bill!
He was on his way to Cairo.
All he could think about was suitcases.

Brave Pete!
He stayed close to his friend.

The Bad Guy put Bill in his garden and went into the house.

"Run me a nice hot tub, Jeeves," the Bad Guy said to his butler. "I will take a bath before dinner. I got me another crocodile today and I need a nap. Call me when the bath is ready."

"Tomorrow that crocodile becomes a suitcase," he added.

"Not if I have anything to say about it," said
Pete. "I'm more than JUST a toothbrush."
And Pete picked the lock with his beak.

"Quick, Bill. Let's get out of here," said Pete.
"No, I'm mad!" said Bill. "I'm going to
make sure there are no more crocodile suitcases."

Bill climbed the wall.

He crept through the living room into the bathroom.

"Your bath is ready, sir," said Jeeves.

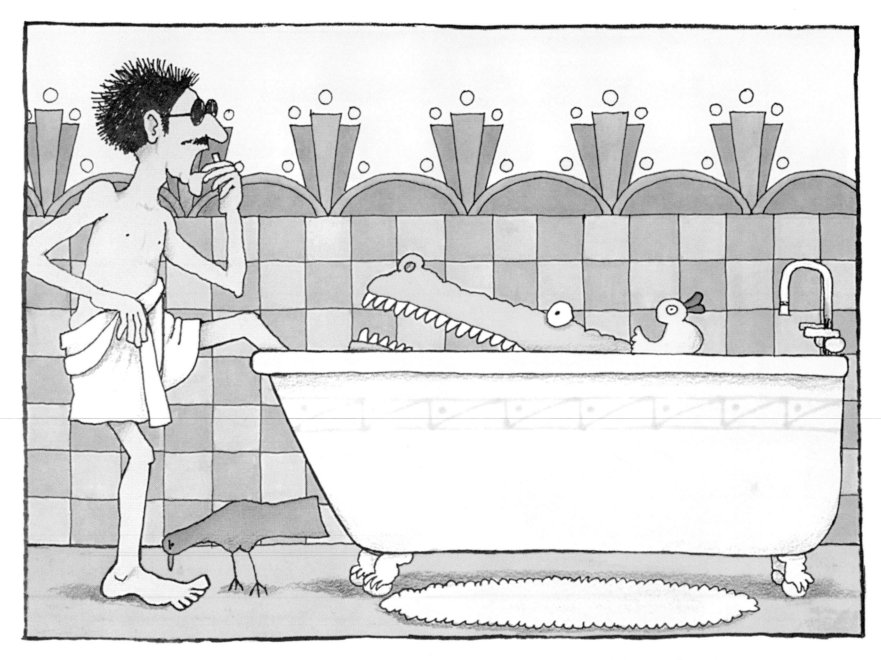

And there was Bill, right with the rubber ducky.

The Bad Guy jumped out of the window
and didn't stop running all the way to Cairo.

"Oh, look, a nice dinner," said Pete.
"And am I hungry," said Bill.

"Mama, you don't have to cook dinner for us tonight," Bill said when they got home. And he told her what had happened.

"Oh, Bill. Oh, Pete," Mama exclaimed.
"What an adventure. I am so proud of the two of you."